The True Spirit of Christmas
Published by P. K. McLemore

SPRINKLES: THE TRUE SPIRIT OF CHRISTMAS

Copyright © 2018, P. K. McLemore

Dedication

I believe in doing what matters. I believe that the spirit of the child within all of us will always prevail. I believe that miracles manifest where hope abounds and that anything is possible. I believe in the power of love, family, and team.

I dedicate "*Sprinkles*" to *Lakisha, Alex, Theo, Connor, Jillian*—my children, it is your gift of love that has kept alive, the spirit of Christmas within me. You inspired and motivated me to create this book, allowing me to share a timeless piece of art with my family and friends each year. I trust that the gift will keep on giving, from your children, to your children's children, and so on.

In presenting this book, I honor my grandfather, the master story teller. It is he who began this tradition when I was young. For that, I am grateful.

I believe that no hurdle in life is meant to be jumped alone. With that, I also dedicate this book to my wonderful wife, *Monika Hill McLemore*, who truly believes there is goodness in all. You bring out the very best in me and have always allowed me to live my dreams without question.

I want to extend a special thanks also, to Ms. Tracie Costello. Thank you for your support and your special cause, The Main Line Animal Rescue. You do believe.

For my readers, I encourage you to embrace the true meaning of Christmas and to always find one hundred thousand reasons to be kind to someone.

Merry Christmas.

Foreword

Kevin McLemore has written a timeless Christmas classic for kids of all ages. *"Sprinkles: The True Sprint of Christmas"* is a story about the bond of family and friendship and most importantly, about the importance of believing in yourself.

The story follows Rudie and a charming cast of characters as they bravely set out on a journey to find Sprinkles, the mystical, magical reindeer who fill the world with the true spirit of Christmas. Along the way, Rudie and his friends encounter many obstacles and dangers, including the menacing Dream Stealers! The Dream Stealers are intent on extinguishing the Ray of Hope, the light that is created from all the hope and dreams that exist in the world.

Rudie, who has the purest of heart, must fight off the Dream Stealers and find Sprinkles before all the Christmas Spirit is gone for good. To save Christmas and to save himself from getting beat up by the class bully, Rudie must dig deep into his heart and believe in himself.

Sprinkles, The True Spirit of Christmas is an engaging and brilliantly descriptive story with a special message, just in time for the holiday that will have you and your loved ones pondering. *Do you Believe?*

Tiffani, Misencik
-Mother, Friend, Reader, and Believer

Contents

SPRINKLES: THE TRUE SPIRIT OF CHRISTMAS

CHAPTER

1

The Birth of Sprinkles

IN THE NORTH POLE, vanilla ice cream scoops of snow dotted the ground, while tiny marshmallow flakes fell steadily from the sky. It was a deliciously magical place, where dreams and toys were gifts for the asking.

On this particular night, just two days before Christmas, a fierce wind was blowing, sending the snow flying in all directions. All of Santa's helpers were tucked away indoors, awaiting the birth of the newest reindeer.

They sat by a fire in a well-lit cave, enjoying the warmth, and talking about the baby being born in the next room. Santa and Mrs. Claus were there, as were a small group of elves and several of the woodland animals. Suddenly they heard a cry and they all jumped up to greet Mrs. Prancer's new baby.

Entering the tiny bedroom, they saw Mrs. Prancer cuddling her newborn reindeer to her chest while Prancer looked on lovingly. A proud father, Prancer turned away so they wouldn't see his tears. But Mrs. Claus reached out and turned him back around.

"Happy tears are always welcomed, my dear," she whispered, kissing his cheek. "Now, let's see the little one."

Mrs. Prancer loosened her arms a bit and Santa rushed up first. "It's a girl!" he exclaimed grandly. "A beautiful little girl."

Sprinkles was tiny, barely bigger than an elf. Her creamy chocolate skin was sprinkled with milky white polka dots. Mrs. Prancer smiled, "We'll call her Sprinkles."

Just as Mrs. Prancer spoke, a light gust of snow swirled through the bedroom, showering Sprinkles' face. She opened her eyes, blinked, and slowly looked at the smiling crowd surrounding her. Her smile was radiant, gleaming brighter than the whitest snow.

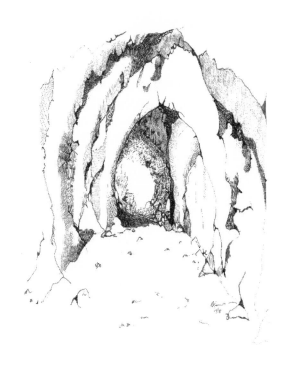

Everyone who looked at her felt their hearts fill with joy and love. But Sprinkles' smile faded suddenly. She closed her eyes and became very still. Everyone gasped.

"What's wrong?" cried Prancer. "She's not moving!"

Mrs. Prancer gently nuzzled her baby, trying to soothe her awake, but nothing happened. Sprinkles was lying there, still as death. Then Santa decided to try. He took Sprinkles in his arms and let his beard tickle her nose. Finally, he looked up, shaking his head sadly, and said, "She's a tiny one, she is. The first reindeer to be born this early."

Santa looked away from Mrs. Prancer, who was crying, and instead, focused on his loyal friend. "I'm sorry, Prancer," he said.

Prancer continued to stare at his baby, letting his wet reindeer tears fall slowly to the floor. By now everyone was crying, and the warm, salty tears were melting the snow-hardened floor of the bedroom.

Just then, the flames from the fire began to rise. And as everyone watched in amazement, one of the embers flew out of the fire and danced slowly around the baby reindeer's small, still body. But this was no ordinary ember. It was an ember called China, *The Princess of Dreams*. She was born in that moment, just to bring Sprinkles back in full spirit.

China put her ear to Sprinkles' chest and heard the soft but steady beat. With a flourish, she reached into a little pouch and sprinkled golden flakes into Sprinkles' lifeless eyes.

"From this day on," whispered China softly, "you will be the heart and soul of all mankind, the very spirit of Christmas. Now wake and spread your love and joy throughout the world."

When China finished, she flew back into the fire and as the flames settled down, Sprinkles opened her eyes and cried. The cry was a tiny one, but it sounded like a symphony to Sprinkles' parents and friends. Tears were replaced with smiles, and everyone clapped and danced. Their hearts once again were filled with love and joy.

Santa twirled around and proclaimed, "Blessed be! Such a tiny thing. Look at those eyes, so blue. They will fill the hearts and souls of all mankind with love and joy." Then he turned to Sprinkles and proclaimed, "Sprinkles, you indeed, are the true spirit of Christmas.

The fire in the little cave burned brightly all night as Sprinkles' friends rejoiced in the little reindeer and her miraculous recovery. They were sure that everyone in the world would be happier, now that Sprinkles was born.

CHAPTER

2

Rudie Believes in Sprinkles

BUT LIFE was not that happy elsewhere in the world. There were lots of people who didn't understand the meaning of Christmas. They were unhappy and had lost their way. Two such people were, at that very moment, sitting in a garbage-filled alley. Their clothes were tattered, they were dirty, and they had no shoes. But most of all, they had no hope.

In fact, all they had between them was one cheap bottle of wine, which they passed back and forth as they sat. The wine was supposed to make them feel better but they felt sadder and sadder as they drank.

As one of the men put the bottle to his lips, he toasted sarcastically, "To Christmas. May this be the happiest of holidays!" Then he took a long swig.

The other man grabbed the bottle, took a big gulp, and replied, "Yeah, whatever." Then they sat. And sat.

The Cunningham house was filled with the sounds of laughter and the smell of freshly baked cookies. The lights from the Christmas tree danced with the light from the television, creating a rainbow-colored two-step that made the small living room as grand as a cathedral.

The Christmas season brought the family together in a very special way. It was very important to Jeff and Angela Cunningham that their three children understood that Christmas was about more than presents. So, on this night, while Angela and Kisha happily baked cookies in the kitchen, Jeff and the boys, Rudie and Junior, watched *The Story of Sprinkles* on television.

Eight-year-old Rudie, who hadn't taken his eyes off the television since the movie began, climbed up onto his father's lap. He asked, "Dad, it's a good thing Sprinkles came to Christmas Town, isn't it? Huh, Dad?"

Jeff put down the newspaper he had been reading and smiled at Rudie. "Yes son, it's a really good thing."

Junior looked over from his perch on the couch, and with a mischievous grin, asked, "Dad, don't you think it's time you told him the—"

Rudie interrupted. "Told me what?"

"Junior!" Jeff yelled menacingly at his oldest son, while Rudie looked from his father to his brother with wide-open eyes.

Rudie opened his mouth to speak, but then Angela walked in with a tray of freshly baked chocolate-chip cookies and stole his attention for the moment.

"How about some hot cookies for Mr. Cold Heart?" Angela asked, addressing Junior.

"Come on, not you too," he replied with a pout.

Jeff spoke to Junior. "Okay, son, you explain this then. Why is it that every year at Christmas you and a lot of other children make an amazing attitude adjustment, suddenly becoming the angels you were meant to be? And folks who never spoke a kind word to you, start to wish you health and happiness?"

Junior hesitated. "What? Well, um, it's just 'cause they—"

"Cause Sprinkles is in their hearts!" Yelled Rudie triumphantly, jumping off his father's lap.

Jeff smiled at his son's enthusiasm. "That little reindeer was born with a heart as pure as gold. Even though she almost lost her way, her spirit was so strong she made it back against terrible odds. Just looking into her eyes makes people feel the true goodness inside themselves."

"Yeah, but she can't be pure all her life," said Junior with a snicker. "She has to grow up sometime."

"That's what made her even more special," Jeff replied. "She never grew up. She stayed young and innocent at heart. Her effect on people grew and multiplied with each passing year. Whenever folks came into contact with her, their hearts immediately filled with love and joy. And as Sprinkles grew wiser, she managed to spread that feeling throughout Christmas Town and the whole world. Especially at Christmas time."

"And that's why Santa called her the true spirit of Christmas."

"That's right, Rudie, that's just the way it happened."

Rudie shot Junior a smug grin. One that said, "See, big brother, I was right."

Out loud he said, "I like that story, dad. It's my favorite. And you always tell it the best. Tell it to me again, please." He smiled pleadingly at Jeff, who patted his always-ready lap.

Just then, Kisha, the oldest of the three children, walked in with a cookie in each hand.

"I like that story too," she mumbled with a mouth full of chocolate chips. "Especially the part when the kids get all that neat stuff."

Against his own will, Junior found himself drawn into the conversation. "My favorite part is when the Dream-Stealers come and suck the dreams out of people's heads."

He pondered about that for a moment. "Hey, maybe that story's not so corny. I wonder if I could get them to suck the brains out of your head, Kisha."

"Now, you two, be nice," Jeff admonished, "or maybe they'll get both of you at the same time."

"Yeah, like a two-for-one," chimed in Rudie. Junior gave him a playful punch on the arm and Kisha threw a pillow at him. Then they all started laughing and eating cookies, and pretty soon it was bedtime.

The next morning in Rudie's third grade class the teacher was late and Sprinkles was the number one topic of conversation. "Hey Pamela," Rudie called to his best friend, "did you watch 'The Spirit of Christmas last night?"

"I would never miss it," she replied excitedly. "He's the cutest reindeer I've ever seen." She pointed to the wall behind the teacher's desk, where someone had thumb-tacked an advertisement for the movie over a poster of Jackie Robinson. "He's much cuter than old Rudolph," she said with a giggle.

Rudie's response was drowned out by the approach of his arch-enemies, Tyrone, Freddy and Skippy. They were the class bullies and the class dummies. They were also overly sensitive about having been left back twice. Everybody in the class was afraid of them, Rudie included. The trio approached with menacing frowns, Tyrone in front as usual. He was the leader, being the biggest, dumbest and meanest. He had greasy black hair, bushy eyebrows and a swagger he picked up in a John Wayne movie.

"Okay, enough baby talk. It's time to pay the man." Tyrone spoke like an apprentice gangster, always trying to imitate the older hoodlums he heard on the street.

Skippy, who was Tyrone's pet puppet, seconded his leader's command. "Yeah, milk money. Give it up! Time to get paid, right Ty?"

Freddy and Skippy approached the other kids, moving quickly before the teacher came in. Tyrone stayed with Rudie and Pamela.

They overheard Freddy saying to one of the little girls, "Come on, come on, you know what they say this time of year. It's better to give than to receive."

Tyrone laughed, but it sounded more like a twisted grunt than a laugh. Rudie handed over his money. "I don't know why you always go around bullying folks."

"It's part of my charm."

15

Pamela, who was very brave, and smarter than anyone else in the class, added sarcastically, "I wonder if being left back twice has anything to do with why you keep taking our milk money every day."

"Pam, you got your facts all wrong," said Skippy, back from his rounds, "only Freddy and I have been left back twice. Ty got left back three times."

Another robbed classmate chimed in. "Wow! Three times! You got to try really hard to accomplish that."

The kids all began to laugh, and Tyrone grabbed Rudie by the front of his shirt. His face was bright red, and he looked like a volcano was ready to explode inside him at any moment. "So you like to laugh? Today you and that little reindeer pay double!"

Tyrone turned to Freddy and Skippy and they nodded their approval. Rudie, still fresh from his wonder with Sprinkles, couldn't resist bringing him up again. "You wouldn't treat folks like this if Sprinkles was any place near that dark heart of yours."

Freddy and Skippy looked at each other in disbelief, then started snickering. "Baby talk, baby talk," said Tyrone. "Rudie Cunningham is in the third grade and still talks baby talk. There's no such thing as Sprinkles or Santa Claus. It's all made up by Hallmark."

"There is too!" cried Rudie, his passion stronger than his fear.

"So prove it."

Tyrone's challenge made the other children draw back. Rudie and Pamela were on their own. But Rudie wasn't afraid because he believed in Sprinkles. "Prove it? Okay, I can do that. Just wait 'til we get back from Christmas break. Yeah, that's it. I'll bring you proof."

"Yeah, and when he does, you got to stop taking our milk money," added Pamela.

Skippy looked panicked. "How are we gonna eat if we don't take their money Ty?"

"Shut up, simple!" barked Tyrone. "He can't prove anything 'cause they're all made-up things."

"Oh, right," agreed Skippy. He was relieved.

Rudie whispered fiercely to Pamela, "Don't help." Then he turned his attention back to Tyrone who was pointing to Rudie and laughing.

"Pay me now or pay me later, it's all the same." Then, Tyrone addressed the rest of the class. "And to all the rest of you little children, if Mr. Rudie Cunningham fails to bring me proof, then all of you will be paying double!"

The children fell silent and stared at Rudie, who stared at the door wondering why the teacher was so late. But he felt the need to show he wasn't afraid. After all, he had been defending himself against Kisha and Junior for years.

He put on a slow pumpkin grin and turned lazily to Tyrone. "Double! Wouldn't you feel better if you went out and got a job?"

Tyrone growled. He knew the other kids were watching. "I said double and double is what I meant. Unless you care to admit right now that Sprinkles doesn't exist. Then things will go back to normal. This is your only out. You better take it before I change my mind."

Rudie stood up as straight as he could, and said with a fake English accent, "Could you please turn your head in another direction? I can't hold my breath much longer."

Rudie laughed along with the other kids, but he was afraid he had gone too far. Still, Tyrone wouldn't hit him in front of the whole class. Would he?

He looked like he might. "Maybe I should just pound you out right now," he yelled, shaking his fist in Rudie's face.

Now Rudie felt really scared, but he tried to hide it with a joke. "Wait! Wouldn't it be better if you pound me later and got double too?"

Tyrone, apparently realizing that he couldn't very well hit Rudie in front of all those witnesses, relented. "I can pound you anytime," he threatened, "but I'll be waiting for your proof."

Tyrone turned and walked away, with Freddy and Skippy close behind. "Better come up with the goods, Cunningham," gibed Freddy.

"Yeah, the goods, yeah," added Skippy.

"Shut up Skippy!" yelled Tyrone and Freddy. Then the three of them walked out of the classroom.

Pamela turned to Rudie and put her arm around his shoulder. "I know you can do it, Rudie," she volunteered.

"Thanks Pam, but don't get crazy with your Christmas fund this year."

CHAPTER

3

Rudie Becomes Frustrated

THAT **AFTERNOON**, as Rudie was leaving school, one of his classmates punched him in the arm and warned, "My financial future is in your hands, Cunningham."

"Thanks," Rudie replied sarcastically. "Just what I need—more pressure."

Rudie sat down on the swings and looked around the schoolyard nervously. What if Tyrone couldn't wait 'til after Christmas break? He seemed like the type of kid who needed to see blood pretty frequently. Rudie wondered what Tyrone's family was like. He imagined a greasy-haired brooding clan with horns and tails. He pictured them punching each other, with squishy red pulp flying through the air. Then he pictured his own family, eating cookies in front of the television, and he groaned.

"It wouldn't even be a fair fight," he said out loud.

"What wouldn't be a fair fight?" asked Junior, who had come with Kisha to pick Rudie up from school.

"Oh nothing. Just something I said got me in trouble today."

"What did you hit them with today?" asked Kisha. "Was it urban reform, or the declining education budget?"

"Yeah," said Junior, a note of annoyance worming into his voice, "how come you know so much stuff? I've been around a lot longer than you, and I don't know half the stuff you talk about."

"I second that," chirped Kisha, pushing Rudie on the swing.

"You too?" asked Junior with surprise.

"No stupid, I meant that I know you don't have the foggiest idea what your little brother is talking about."

"Like you do?"

"I didn't say I did, but I'm not saying I don't either."

Junior stuck out his tongue and crossed his eyes. Kisha blew him a kiss.

"Hey," Rudie complained. "At what point does the concern come back to the kid with the problem? Tyrone wants double the money from everyone now and it's all my fault."

"I don't get it," sighed Junior. "In my day, the school bully never asked for a raise. Times sure have changed."

Rudie gave him a dirty look and turned his attention to Kisha. "Well, we won't have to pay him anything ever again if I can prove to him that Sprinkles is real."

With a wink at Junior, Kisha ignored Rudie's last comment. "So, do you have to pay these guys weekly or is there some deferred plan you can take?" she asked, barely stifling a laugh.

Rudie jumped off the swing in disgust. "Why do I ever talk to you two? I needed some intelligent advice and what do I get? *Dumb* and her kid brother *Real Stupid.*"

"Come on Rudie, come back," called Kisha, but Rudie ran as fast as he could out of the schoolyard. Then, he came back in through an entrance on the other side so Junior and Kisha wouldn't find him if they came looking.

He laid down in the cold grass and stared up at the grey clouds that swirled furiously around the pale-yellow sun. He closed his eyes and focused his brain on the problems at hand. *Is Sprinkles real, and if so, how do I prove it? Am I nuts? Am I going to get killed after Christmas break? Was I adopted or are my brother and sister just morons?*

All those questions made him tired and he fell asleep. He dreamt about Tyrone and how Santa Claus wouldn't bring him any more toys. When he woke, he was shivering, and a pale pink light in the sky was the only thing saving him from total darkness and tears. He jumped up quickly and ran home, wondering if Kisha and Junior had told their parents what had happened.

He opened the front door cautiously, ready with an excuse if one was needed. But nobody jumped out at him, nobody demanded an explanation.

"Pretty sweet," he thought to himself, "maybe my siblings have one or two redeeming qualities after all." As he tiptoed past the living room, he heard his name and walked inside.

"Good evening son. Kisha told me you were out playing with your friend Jake this afternoon."

"She told you that? I mean, yeah, we just hung out as his house. Where's mom?"

"She went shopping. She'll be back soon. Go do your homework."

CHAPTER
4

Clumsy Junior

AFTER A DELICIOUS DINNER of fried chicken, sweet potatoes and homemade buttermilk biscuits, Rudie climbed onto his father's lap and pushed aside the newspaper he was reading.

"So what are you doing?"

"I believe I was reading," Jeff replied warily.

Rudie continued. "What were you reading? Anything you want to talk about?"

Jeff got it. "No, Rudie. Is there anything you want to talk about?"

"Well, since you asked. You're up on everything, right?"

Jeff laughed. Sometimes it was very nice being a father. "Most of the time I am. Why?"

Rudie got very serious. He stared into his father's eyes. "We can talk man-to-man, can't we Dad?"

"Sure son. No problem."

Still staring hard into his father's eyes, Rudie asked, "You would tell me if something wasn't true, wouldn't you?"

"Yes."

"So the story about Sprinkles and Christmas Town is true, isn't it? Huh, Dad, huh?"

"Well, do you think it's true?" Jeff asked.

"Of course I do!"

Jeff dropped his newspaper to the floor and pulled Rudie close. "Remember what I told you? If there's something you believe in, nobody has the right to try to make you feel differently."

"I wish Tyrone knew that," responded Rudie glumly.

"Who's Tyrone?"

"He's kind of like the class financial consultant."

"You mean the class bully," confirmed Jeff, nodding his head. "We had those when I was your age too. So what happened?"

"Nothing really. I was talking with Pamela about Sprinkles, and Tyrone and his friends overheard. They started to tease me, saying there was no such thing as Santa or Sprinkles and that the whole story was made up to trick little kids into feeling good about themselves. I told him he didn't know what he was talking about."

"So what did he say?" Jeff was very interested, having had his own run-ins with a class bully some thirty years earlier. He was proud of Rudie for sticking up for himself, but he was worried too.

Just then, Junior walked by, his hands filled with cookies. "Said he needed more cash to support his early childhood career in crime," he shouted, on his way to the den.

Rudie and his father exchanged rolled eyes and resumed their conversation. "I didn't want to look bad in front of the other kids," Rudie continued, "so I told him that I would prove it. That's when he said if I didn't, he wanted double his money—and not just from me—from the whole class."

"You'll pay him nothing!" Jeff shouted.

"You want to tell Tyrone that? Come on, Dad. Just help me get the proof. Okay?"

Saved by a loud crash, Jeff didn't have to respond. He and Rudie jumped up to investigate. They found Junior in the den standing amid broken glass and broken cookies.

"I didn't do it," he protested, before anyone said a word. "I got here just before you did."

"Junior, that vase was brand-new. I just bought it for your mother's birthday."

"Yeah, it was nice," said Junior.

Jeff threw up his hands in exasperation. "Just pick up this mess and then off to bed. Maybe a few things will be spared if you're asleep."

He walked out of the room and Rudie followed. "Hey, Rudie. Where are you going? Give me a hand, will ya?" begged Junior.

Rudie didn't turn around. He needed to talk to his mom. He followed the cookie smell to the kitchen. More cookies. Fresh cookies. Christmas was the best!

Red and white Santa cookies were cooling on a tray when Rudie walked in. "Hey mom, you make the best cookies in town," he complimented, grabbing a handful that had already cooled. "You should write a cookbook or something."

"Thank you," Angela replied, wiping the sweat from her upper lip with the dishtowel she had wrapped around her waist. "But I didn't get a Master's Degree in Psychology to become Aunt Jemima. I think I've baked enough cookies to last the rest of the year."

"I know," agreed Rudie, kissing her cheek.

"Now run off, you, I'm exhausted and I have to clean up before I can drag myself off to bed."

Rudie hesitated, then kissed her again. "Goodnight Mom."

"Goodnight. Kiss, kiss. Love you."

Rudie walked to his bedroom, determined to get a good night's sleep. He was not going to worry about stupid Tyrone all night. When he got there, Junior was already in bed and Jeff was checking his homework. After he checked Rudie's homework, he kissed both of them goodnight and turned off the lights.

"Good night boys. The angel of the night will watch over you while you sleep." Then he went to say goodnight to Kisha.

Later that night, Kisha was awakened by a loud crash and woke to find Junior standing next to her bed. She screamed. "J-u-n-i-o-r!"

"I didn't do it. I swear. I didn't do it." Junior's familiar refrain filled the already broken silence.

"Junior Cunningham, if I find that you accidentally broke something of mine, I'm going to accidentally break your neck!"

Junior was about to repeat his innocence when they heard their Dad's voice thundering from downstairs. "I want everyone asleep now! Do I make myself clear?"

Junior scrambled back to his room, but he was unable to sleep. Rudie was also unable to sleep because Junior kept up a steady stream of chatter. Finally, in desperation, Rudie called out to Jeff for a glass of water. "Me too," yelled Junior.

A few minutes later, their weary father trudged into their bedroom with two glasses of water and a stern face. "Now, you drink this and then not another peep out of either of you."

"No problem, Dad," they replied in unison. But then Junior reached for Rudie's glass and in the process, knocked over both glass and night stand. Jeff came running back in, steaming.

"I didn't do it," moaned Junior, crossing his heart. You've gotta to believe me this time. I didn't do it, I swear."

"So who did it? Did a little man appear out of nowhere?"

Junior jumped at his Dad's suggestion. "Wow, dial the psychic hotline! That's just what happened. See, this little man, you know the one Dad, he came in through

31

the window, and I guess he got a little thirsty, and Rudie's glass was just sitting there nice and cold and filled almost to the top."

"That's enough son."

"Dad, you got to hear me out," Junior pleaded. "I'm telling the truth this time. He went for Rudie's water and I tried to stop him, and that's when he broke the nightstand and jumped back out the window. I would have caught him, but he got a good head start and he was really fast. But if we'd been even Steven, I would have caught him, and none of this would have happened, and you wouldn't be looking at me like that."

Jeff shook his head in disbelief but was too tired to argue. "Okay, if that's what happened, it's over now. Go to sleep, and if anyone else comes into your room, just let him have whatever he wants and maybe he won't break anything." He looked around the room as if checking for a strange little man then said goodnight and left.

CHAPTER

5

Going to Christmas Town

SOME TIME LATER, a strange light began to fly around the room, flickering close to Rudie. Junior was fast asleep, but Rudie had lain awake thinking about Tyrone.

"Rudie, I need your help."

Rudie answered what he thought was Junior's voice. "I'm trying to sleep. I'll help you tomorrow, okay?"

The light danced bright circles around Rudie's face to capture his attention. "Now, Rudie!" she ordered in her high, thin voice.

Rudie sat up, wide awake. "Wait a minute. Get that light out of my eyes." He still thought it was Junior.

"Shhh," whispered the light, "you'll wake everyone."

Now Rudie realized what was happening. "God, I must be losing it. A talking light?"

"I really need your help, Rudie. Please come with me," the light implored, ignoring his confusion.

"Wait a minute. What's wrong with this picture? Lights don't talk. Who are you? What are you?"

Just as the light had feared, Rudie woke Junior, who called out sleepily for Rudie to be quiet. Rudie looked at him, already asleep again after speaking, then back at the light that was hovering near him.

"I've got to be dreaming," he said softly. "This is too weird to be real. Maybe if I close my eyes I'll dream about something else."

"Rudie, this isn't a dream. I'm real. Come on, we're wasting time." The light got brighter.

Rudie finally came to his senses. "I can't go with you," he told the light. "I don't know who or what you are, and besides, I have to ask my Dad's permission before I leave the house."

"I'm China, the Princess of Dreams," the light explained. "I've been watching you for a long time, and you're the only one who can help me."

Rudie stopped now to take a good look at China. She had wings like an angel but otherwise looked like a fairy tale version of Wonder Woman. She wore a bright blue outfit, white boots and a gold tiara. She looked strong, like someone who was used to getting her way, yet nice. She also looked like someone who used her powers only for good.

"But why me? I'm just a kid, what can I do?" he asked, secretly flattered.

"What I need is somebody with a pure heart. Yours is so clean it sparkles. Trust me Rudie, you stand out from all the others. And for what I need you to do, we're going to need everything you have in that heart of yours to keep you safe from the Dream-Stealers."

Rudie became excited when he heard about the Dream-Stealers. He remembered them from the Christmas story, how they stole people's dreams in order to make them lose the Christmas spirit.

As if reading Rudie's mind, China added, "Just like in the story. Now hurry, we don't have much time left if we're going to find Sprinkles and bring her back to Christmas Town in time for Christmas. And if we don't find her, the spirit of Christmas will be lost, and the world will be a dark and lonely place forever."

It was a big responsibility for a little boy. "You picked me to help?" Rudy asked, still somewhat in shock.

"Are you coming now or what?" asked China, losing her patience.

Rudie threw up his hands. "What choice do I have? You talk and fly, and who knows what else. So I guess I'm in."

Rudie leapt out of bed, threw on his jeans, sneakers and a Cleveland Indian's baseball jacket, and looked at China for a command. She led him to his closet.

Rudie stopped short, suddenly rethinking his heroism. "Wait, that's my closet," he protested, "I'm not going in there without the light of day. I've lost three pairs of my best Nikes to the beast who lives there at night."

As China tried to push Rudie into the closet, the noise woke Junior again. "Hey Rudie, where are you going?"

"Got something to do. Go back to sleep."

"Can't it wait 'til morning?"

"Keep it down," said Rudie, putting his finger to his lips, "I'll be back soon."

Now Junior was really awake. He finally noticed China, and started yelling. "Where do you think you're going? And what is that?"

Juniors' yelling woke Kisha who ran into the room, also yelling. "Hey, what's with all the noise? Some of us

37

normal people are trying to get some sleep." Then she saw Rudie. "And Mr. Rudie Cunningham, where do you think you're going all dressed up?"

"Christmas Town."

"You've got to be nuts. I wonder if Mom and Dad know you're running off to Christmas Town with that light flying around your head." She stopped, momentarily dumbfounded, and just stared at China. She rubbed her eyes, closed them and opened them again.

"A talking light? Oh my God!" she yelled frantically. "I'm going to get Dad. He'll help you. Stay right here. I'll –"

"–Kisha wait!" Rudie grabbed Kisha's arm and tried to stop her from leaving the room. I'm okay. China needs me. Just please keep it down. I swear I'm okay."

China saw her opportunity and began to pull Rudie into the closet. Rudie grabbed onto the door, but then gave up, and let China have him. "I hope the bogeyman doesn't have a taste for fairies," he told her, "cause if he shows up you're on your own."

As China pulled Rudie deeper into the closet, she lit up with radiant colors of red, blue, pink and yellow. Ahead of them a wall opened up and the colors were out there too. It was a rainbow world, and Rudie could just barely glimpse it through the opening.

China looked at Rudie calmly for the first time. "Just hold onto me and jump."

Rudie was excited by the colors, but still a little nervous. "This Christmas Town doesn't come with its own bogeyman, does it?" he asked with a short laugh.

"Just jump," China ordered.

As Rudie and China jumped, Kisha and Junior finally sprang into action. Kisha reached in and grabbed Rudie's arm, preventing his descent into Christmas Town. "Don't worry little brother, I have you now. Junior! How about a little help?"

Rudie struggled to break free from Kisha, but Junior was now helping her. Junior grabbed onto the doorknob for more leverage. It was the doorknob and Junior and Kisha against China in a life or death tug of war for Rudie. But Rudie wanted to go with China and was trying to help her as much as he could by twisting and squirming away from Kisha.

Just then, a baseball bat fell down off the wall and hit Junior's hand, causing him to let go of the nearly broken doorknob. All four of them tumbled through the opening, into the brightness that was Christmas Town.

CHAPTER

6

Meeting Santa

RUDIE, CHINA, JUNIOR, AND KISHA landed together in Christmas Town, thrown together in a room so dark, the only thing visible was the whites of their eyes. There was a dank, putrid odor as if garbage had been rotting for weeks in the hot sun. It sure didn't feel like Christmas Town.

Kisha was the first to regain her composure. "Something smells bad in Cleveland," she whimpered, wiggling her nose in disgust. "Junior, are your shoes on your feet?"

Still pretty shaken, Junior retorted, "This isn't Cleveland and my feet never smelled this bad."

He laughed but then it got quiet again. Real quiet. Kisha shivered and reached out for Rudie. "I don't like the dark," she whispered. "Bad things happen in dark places. I want to go home. I want to go back to my room now!" Her voice rose shrilly, as if she were about to cry.

Luckily, they were saved by China, who was finally able to straighten out her wings and fly. As she did, her light grew brighter and brighter. The children reached out for each other. "Where are we?" asked Rudie nervously.

"Unless your family has thrown us off course," responded China, shooting disapproving looks at Kisha and Junior, "we should be somewhere at the North Pole near Christmas Town."

"But what if we're not?" asked Kisha, still fighting back tears.

China laughed softly. "You know that bogeyman you were so worried about?"

"Yeah..." answered Rudie.

"Start to worry."

At that, the children started to mobilize, searching for a way out of the darkness. It seemed at first, that the only glow was coming from China, but then Rudie discovered a sliver of pale pink light which seemed to be coming from a doorway. They all looked at each other, wondering if they should go for it.

Junior decided to take charge and ran toward the light. As Kisha reached out to stop him, Junior grabbed her, and then accidentally hooked Rudie and China too. Kisha and Rudie tried to pull Junior back, grabbing onto his arms and then his legs. Junior was strong but all the pulling and grabbing made him lose his balance. He tripped, and when he landed, he was on the other side of the doorway.

The other side of the doorway turned out to be the living room of Santa and Mrs. Claus. At that moment, they were sitting side-by-side, drinking hot chocolate and reading letters. As always, they wore matching red outfits trimmed in white fur. But that's where the resemblance ended. Santa's long hair was pulled back into a ponytail and he wore an earring in his right ear. Mrs. Claus remained more traditional, with pearls and a bright purple apron tied around her waist.

The Claus' living room was very bright, with golden yellow walls and bright red carpeting. It was easy to be both peaceful and happy there. When China and the children tumbled in, Santa and Mrs. Claus jumped off their chairs in amazement, knocking both cups of hot chocolate to the floor.

Rudie spoke first. "We're sorry. We didn't mean to startle you, but –"

" – China, who are these people?" Santa interrupted. "Why, my goodness, there's three of them."

China looked at him sheepishly. "I meant to bring just the one, but..." She trailed off, not knowing how to explain what happened. "It was an accident," she said finally.

"We didn't mean to just drop in like this," offered Rudie again.

Santa beamed his big Santa smile. "That's okay, little one. I'm sure it's no trouble at all."

Mrs. Claus asked the children their names and everyone relaxed. Santa had a whispered conversation with China, and as they spoke, a small group of elves gathered in the doorway and stared at the children. Kisha finally realized where they were.

"Am I right?" she asked incredulously. "You're the Mr. and Mrs. Claus? The folks with the sleigh and eight tiny reindeer and all that?"

"Yes we are," replied Santa, nodding at the elves.

Kisha's eyes lit up and she ran to Santa and hugged him. "Then you got my list, right? You couldn't have missed it. It was the one with all the pretty pink ribbons on it." She turned to Mrs. Claus. "I did that so he'd read mine first."

Santa's eyes started to tear. "Yes, I've seen your letter."

"What's wrong?" asked Kisha. "My list wasn't too long, was it? I could make some adjustments if that would make you feel better."

"No child, your list is fine. I just wish there was more time; we need more time." Santa absentmindedly patted Kisha's head as he looked at Mrs. Claus.

"Is there anything we can do to help?" asked Rudie.

"What do you mean we?" whispered Junior fiercely.

Santa was still patting Kisha's head when he answered. "I'm sorry to be so sad, but since Sprinkles has been gone, Christmas Town just hasn't been the same." He pressed a button on the wall and a screen appeared. "Look at this," he said, motioning with his hand.

The screen came to life with thousands of people all over the world looking hopeless and sad. Children were crying, women were sighing, men were fighting. Even the flowers and trees looked wilted and droopy. From Brazil to Bangkok, California to the Caribbean, New York to New Delhi, the world was losing its Christmas spirit.

Santa continued. "I don't think the world will ever be the same if we don't get Sprinkles back before Christmas Eve. After all, what would Christmas be without the Christmas spirit?"

SPRINKLES: THE TRUE SPIRIT OF CHRISTMAS

Mrs. Claus told the children Sprinkles' story. Of course, they knew it already, but it was much more special to hear it from Mrs. Claus and they paid rapt attention. She reminded them how Sprinkles brought happiness and joy to everyone she touched, how she was the good in everything, and how this was especially true at Christmas time.

While Mrs. Claus was speaking, China was flying around Santa, anxious to hear her own part in Sprinkles' story. Santa told the children, "It was Sprinkles who gave life to China, who deemed her the Princess of Dreams." He sighed a long sigh. "She was our light and now I fear she may be lost forever."

Mrs. Claus was crying, and Kisha reached for her hand. "Don't worry," she reassured her. "If you really believe that Rudie and that light are your only hope, then they'll find her. Junior and I will go along to back them up. You just tell Santa to keep an eye on my list." Kisha looked at Rudie and smiled broadly. She didn't feel scared any more.

"Rudie Cunningham," she shouted gleefully, "Let's put this show on the road!"

CHAPTER

7

A Night in the Cave

SANTA WANTED THE CHILDREN to wait until the morning but they were determined to find Sprinkles as quickly as possible. So Santa pointed them in the right direction and sent one of his elves to follow from a distance, in case they needed help.

As soon as they stepped out of Santa's house, China and the children found themselves in a snow-filled forest, a wonderland of tall bare trees covered with frosted creamy vanilla. Snow sculptures depicting Santa and the reindeer, dotted their path like cookie crumbs, ensuring they wouldn't get lost. And so China flew, and the children walked, and they were all excited and caught up in their fairy tale adventure.

Nobody spoke until they came down a snow-covered mountain to find the grass and trees green as summer, the air warm and buzzing with a fragrant spring breeze. They all stopped at once, amazed by the change.

Rudie spoke first. "Everything here is so perfect. It seems almost unreal."

"It's like in a storybook," agreed Kisha, bending to pick up a daisy.

Then Junior spotted something in the distance, a small form seated on the grass. He thought it might be Sprinkles. "Hey, look over there," he cried, "this little adventure could be over before it's begun."

But it wasn't. It was a little boy, wearing a loose red robe, wooden sandals and a flat red hat.

He looked very sad, sitting alone on his straw mat. Kisha approached him, but he didn't look up. Even when she waved her hand in his face, he sat motionlessly. Rudie was all set to tap his shoulder, when a voice spoke up behind them.

"Excuse me. I'll check him out."

Rudie, Junior and Kisha turned in surprise and spoke in unison. "Who are you?"

"I'm one of Santa's helpers," the elf who spoke replied. "I'm sure you've read about us. My name is Wiggles."

"Well then, Wiggles, shouldn't you be back there helping Santa with all that Christmas stuff?" asked Rudie.

"Nah, not much is happening at the big house since Sprinkles disappeared. Anyway, I miss her too much. We used to hang out a lot and talk about how nice it would be to meet people like you, but so much bad stuff goes on in the world. I don't think Sprinkles could handle it."

"So she ran away?" asked Rudie.

"Nah, she wouldn't do that."

"So what happened to her?" asked Kisha.

"Dream-Stealers."

The children looked at each other in confusion. Of course, they'd heard of the Dream-Stealers, but were they real? Wiggles went on to describe them.

"I don't quite know who they are," he began, "because they take on many forms. All I know is that as soon as there's any doubt in your heart they start to chip away at you. Dream-Stealer number 3 comes in and multiplies that doubt.

Then Dream-Stealer number 2 implants regret. Finally, Dream-Stealer number 1 creates a hopelessness so deep there's almost no chance of returning. They chip and chip and chip until you're so far off the course that you don't know if you're coming or going."

He stopped and then gestured to the still motionless boy. "Now are we going to sit here and talk, or do you want me to check the stiff?"

Answering himself, Wiggles lightly touched the boy's shoulder and asked if he was alive. In one swift motion the boy grabbed Wiggles' hand and twisted his wrist. "One must not touch unless one wants to be touched," he warned, his eyes still closed.

"Ouch! That hurts!" cried Wiggles.

"Let him go," pleaded Rudie. "We only want to talk to you."

The boy released Wiggles and slowly opened his eyes. "So sorry, but one never knows." He gave a slight bow. "I am Hem Wong."

"Hey, I know what you mean," said Junior, "I'm wrong most of the time too."

"No, my slightly-smart friend, my name is Hem Wong."

Kisha asked Hem Wong if he had seen Sprinkles. He gave a strange reply. "I meditate in this very peaceful place every day. But the feeling that used to be here, the one that relaxed me, is no longer here."

"Is that yes or no?" asked Kisha impatiently.

"What part of no did my poorly-dressed flower not get?" asked Hem Wong.

"Now Wong," said Rudie, "it wasn't nice to smart off like that. She just asked if - "

" - I know what she asked. I answered the only way Wong knows. If Wong upset her, then I am so sorry."

The children exchanged glances. Rudie scowled at Wong. "I'm sure that we would all like to stay here all day and play word games with you, but we don't have much time to find Sprinkles."

"The spirit of Christmas will be lost forever if she doesn't come back," added China with a wail.

"Oh no, I could not let that happen," said Hem Wong with another bow, "If you please, I would like to join your search."

"I'm okay with it," said Rudie, "the more, the merrier. Let's go!"

And off they went, more determined than ever to find Sprinkles. But what they didn't know, is that three figures began to follow them from a distance. Three ominous figures.

Eventually, the little group came upon a town, or what was left of one. It looked like it had been deserted for years, and untouched snow lay piled like laundry in doorways and on windowsills.

It was cold, quiet, and eerie. The only sign of life came from a water pump that was spitting water from its spout. But who could have turned it on? The children drew a little closer together and stared at the flowing water in silence.

Hem Wong finally spoke. "Town looks like no one pay rent on time," he said in his cryptic way.

"Yeah, like no one is here," added Junior.

"That's what I said." Wong gave Junior a dirty look.

Wiggle's spoke up. "Dudes, my little legs need a rest. If the folks that lived here are no longer, maybe we should make like smoke and blow."

"Maybe those Dream-Stealers got them too," whispered Kisha nervously.

Even though they were afraid, everyone agreed they had to look for Sprinkles. Besides, they were hungry and hoped to find some food. So they split up and began ringing doorbells and peering through windows. Just as they were beginning to lose hope, a snowball whizzed through the air and hit Kisha in the back.

"Hey Junior!" she cried.

Then another snowball came, and this time it hit China, knocking her to the ground. Suddenly the air was filled with tiny, enemy snowballs. They came from every direction, hitting the children and the others.

"Quick everyone, take cover! We're being attacked!" yelled Rudie. He ran behind a well and Wong and Wiggles ducked behind a house. China was still in shock, and flew unsteadily around Rudie's head. Kisha stood still, more worried about her wet hair than the unseen attackers.

But Junior refused to give in. "Stop!" he shouted to the group, "If they want a fight, then let's give them one!"

He reached down to the snow, packed a snowball, and threw. Then he did it again... and again... and again. Having no visible target, he just threw snowballs in every direction, hoping for a hit. The rest of the group got excited too and came out of hiding to throw snowballs. Even Kisha got involved, although many of her snowballs mysteriously landed on Junior.

Wiggles turned to Wong and admitted, "This is the fiercest battle I've ever been in."

"I find it rather stimulating," replied Wong. It wasn't long though, before a snowball hit him squarely in the face. "That I don't like," he said with a frown.

Pretty soon the air was white with flying snowballs, and the children were worn out and hot from the effort. All at once they started laughing; giant, wide-open belly laughs. First Rudie, then Kisha, then Junior, even Wiggles and Wong soon collapsed in uncontrollable fits of laughter.

"I can't stop laughing!" yelled Rudie.

"Me either!" yelled Kisha.

"This is the best!" yelled Junior.

"Yeah, it's a real blast," agreed Rudie. Then he stopped mid-laugh. A thousand of tiny furballs were coming toward them from every direction, laughing as loud as the children. "Uh, what are they?" asked Rudie, turning to China.

"They're covered with fur!" exclaimed Kisha.

By now the laughing furballs surrounded the little group. Rudie looked at China again, although he wasn't afraid.

"I don't know, Rudie. I've never seen these creatures before."

"Anyone have any ideas?" asked Kisha. "They're everywhere. What are they? What are they going to do with us?"

"Don't worry Kisha," advised Junior. "Nothing's going to eat you. I don't think they want to get sick."

"Junior!"

"Stop it, you two," said Rudie. "Look. They're coming closer."

As the furballs approached, Rudie and the others could see that their pink and white fur covered every part of their bodies except for a small patch on their heads. They had freshwater blue eyes, so sparkly that the children laughed with joy just to look at them. Nobody was afraid.

Two of the furballs approached Rudie, and not knowing what to do, he extended his hand. "I don't know if you understand me," he said awkwardly, "but we won't hurt you."

The furballs just looked at Rudie's hand and giggled. He started to feel uncomfortable. "What's so funny?" he asked. "Can you talk? Why are you laughing at us?"

Finally one of them spoke. "Yes we understand," he said with a smile, "we speak many languages."

Then he introduced himself as Yunnie, and his friend as Matt. "Pardon us for laughing," said Matt, "but that's what we do."

"Why?" asked Rudie.

"We don't really know," Yunnie replied. "We don't live too long, so we try to have as much fun as we can while we're here."

Having finally overcome her shock, Kisha walked over to Yunnie and tried to touch his bald spot. "I wouldn't do that if I were you," warned Matt.

"Why not? It's kind of neat," said Kisha, still trying to touch it. She pointed to Yunnie's head. "It's a perfect circle."

"We never touch that spot," explained Yunnie. "We hope that if we leave it alone the fur will grow back. All of us have it. All of the men, that is."

He went on to explain, "I think it started with our ancestors who wore those little caps on their heads. Over the years, the hair just stopped growing there."

"Cleveland fan, huh?" asked Junior.

"Much worse," replied Matt, "Yankees."

Everybody had a good laugh, but then China turned to Rudie and reminded him why they were there. She explained to Yunnie and Matt that they had come to look for Sprinkles.

Yunnie nodded and smiled. "Ah, Sprinkles. The littlest reindeer, we knew her well."

As Yunnie and Matt described some of the fun times they'd had with Sprinkles, the three shadowy figures in the distance moved a little closer. It was the Dream-Stealers, trying to prevent the children from finding Sprinkles.

"Let's get them now," said Dream-Stealer number.

"No, I've got plans for them later," responded Dream-Stealer number 1, with a grimace. "Big plans."

They stayed out of sight, but the children felt an eerie presence, like a cold wind that swirled out of nowhere.

Kisha looked around uneasily. "I feel like someone's watching us."

"It's been like that ever since those monsters came through our town a few days ago," agreed Matt.

Kisha looked at Matt as if he were a monster, and began pacing back and forth. "Monsters? Nobody ever said anything about any monsters when I signed up for this trip." Kisha's face was alternately white with fear and red with determination. She walked in circles, talking to herself.

"Got to get out of here. I didn't know when I came along to find Mr. Fix-Everything Little Reindeer that I would have anything to do with monsters."

She raced over to Rudie and bent close to his face. "I want out of here and I mean NOW!" she shouted. Then she ran over to China. "Okay Missy, get me out of here. Beam me up or whatever it is you do but put me back in my own room." Kisha finally stopped moving, and stood with hands on hips, staring at China.

"I'm sorry Kisha, but I can't send you back. I had only enough power to bring Rudie here.

When you and Junior came along, you drained my reserves. My power will be restored now only if Rudie finds Sprinkles." China's speech left everyone else speechless. Junior and Kisha both turned to Rudie with mean scowls.

Rudie threw up his hands and half-smiled. "Hey guys, it's me, your little brother. Come on, it's not my fault you're here. You wanted to come." He paused. "Didn't you?"

Hem Wong spoke up. "Perhaps it's not as bad as it seems."

"And what's that supposed to mean?" asked Kisha, still growling. "If you cannot get back to your little world unless you find Sprinkles - "

"—Yeah?" interrupted Rudie.

"Then you must find the little reindeer," concluded Hem Wong with a bow.

Surprisingly, Junior agreed. He grabbed Rudie's hand and said, "Hem Wong is right. We're wasting time just standing here. Let's get a move on. I want to be home for Christmas dinner."

Junior's enthusiasm was contagious and soon all the children banded together with renewed hope, laughing and cheering and determined to find Sprinkles.

Yunnie and Matt decided to come along and soon the whole merry group was on its way. But not far behind, the Dream Stealers watched and waited, and planned.

As the group continued to walk, the sky turned crimson-black and a polar wind swirled monstrous fanged flakes around them. They knew they had to stop and find shelter, but had only China's light to cut a weak path through the storm. Eventually, just as her strength was giving out, China spotted a cave buried under the snow.

Hem Wong peered in the cave and stepped back. "May I speak?" he asked. "This looks to me to be a dark and empty cave, not what I expected when we sought shelter."

"It's getting really cold out here," said Kisha, hugging herself as tight as she could, "I don't think we have much choice."

"Yo, maybe this is the home of something that hasn't eaten yet and we're the late-night snack," said Wiggles.

"Yeah," agreed Kisha, ready again to take her chances outdoors, "What if the monster lives here?"

Rudie stood in front of the cave entrance and folded his arms across his chest. "It's too cold out here to argue the what-ifs. The storm's not letting up. One of us has to go in and check out this cave."

Everyone turned and looked at Junior. "Oh no, not me," he said, backing away. "I've seen this before; send in the one you don't mind losing. You guys need someone who wants to be a hero."

Wiggles, waist-high in snow by now, couldn't stand it anymore. "Yo dude, I got your back," he told Junior. "It's either get eaten by whatever's inside or stand here and become a popsicle."

"I'll go too," volunteered Yunnie.

At this point Junior couldn't back down without looking like a coward, so he straightened himself up as tall as he could and entered the cave. "You guys know that if I don't make it back, you'll all have to live with this forever, right?"

The group shrugged and Junior walked inside. But China began to get nervous. "The storm is getting worse," she said. "We can't wait out here for another minute. We have to go in -- NOW!" Nobody moved, but then a tree fell nearby from the force of the wind and scared everyone so much that they followed Junior into the cave without another word. They walked into a dark cave, darker than their scariest nightmares.

"Maybe this wasn't such a good idea," said Rudie.

"Just stay together," whispered China. "We'll be okay."

"Shhh," whispered Junior, "Did you hear that?"

The children shook their heads and looked around the dark cave.

"There it goes again," said Junior.

"I don't hear anything," said Rudie. You must have had your bells rung once too often and now they're ringing on their own."

"This is no joke, Rudie," Junior insisted. "There's something or someone in here. I can hear it calling my name."

"If someone's calling you out here, it's got to be a wrong number," said Kisha.

"Someday I'm going to put your face on TV then change the channel."

"And by the time you figure out how to use the remote there will be world peace."

"Stop it, you two," yelled Rudie. "We can't keep wasting time with all this fighting. Christmas will be here soon and we know what happens if we don't find Sprinkles. So let's check out this cave, get some rest, and continue our search tomorrow."

Kisha and Junior both stopped, surprised at the authority in their baby brother's voice. "Rudie's right," added China, "It's dark in here, but it seems safe. Let's just settle down for the night."

"It's a little cold in here," said Kisha, still hugging herself. "Maybe we could build a fire?"

"I know, Junior gets the firewood," said Junior.

He left with Yunnie and Wiggles while the rest of the group gathered leaves and branches to make beds for themselves. Eventually a fire was lit and beds were made and everyone except Junior settled down snugly and went to sleep. Junior lay awake, still hearing his name being called softly from the air.

"Who's there?" he asked nervously. "I know you're there. I can hear you calling my name."

He cocked his head, waiting for an answer. He spoke again, a little more forcefully. "Come on, speak to me already. Show your face or leave me alone."

Finally he got so frustrated he sat up and shook his fist at the air. Then he sank back down and pulled the covers over his head. Maybe Kisha was right. Maybe he was crazy after all.

Just then the voice spoke to him. "Junior, you're not crazy," it said in a deep bass.

"You said it again. You said my name!" Junior threw the covers off and sat up straight. "Please come out and show yourself. Please."

Junior stopped and thought for a moment. "Unless you're really ugly and eat little boys for late night snacks," he added.

"Relax, Junior. I'm not as scary as I sound. And I'm sorry for teasing you."

"But why can't I see you?"

"Let me introduce myself," the voice answered. "I am the North Wind. How do you do?" "Fine, I think," responded Junior.

"What am I doing?" he asked out loud. "I've got to be nuts. I'm having a conversation with the wind? Maybe if I go to sleep, this will all go away."

"I'll be here," the North Wind intoned.

Junior still wasn't sure if the North Wind was a friend or an enemy. He began speaking rapidly, as much to himself as to the voice. "Why me? What did I do? I know I've knocked over a thing or two in my time, and maybe I pick on my sister and brother a little, but my dad says everything will work out okay. He says I'll be a great artist like him someday, but that for now I should relax and be a kid for as long as possible."

Junior looked up into the air. "So whatever this is, it's just a growing-up mistake. Okay?"

The North Wind made a clucking noise. "Life's tough, huh kid?"

"You have no idea."

"I understand. I know growing up can be tough at times. That's why I've chosen to help you."

"What makes you think I need your help?" asked Junior, a little of his bravado back now that he knew the voice wasn't going to eat him.

The North Wind laughed an odd sound like a drumbeat. "I was young once too, the center of attention in my family. Then my sisters, Spring and Summer, came along and everyone liked them better. They were cool; I was messy. I felt unnoticed so I did a few things to remind the folks I was still around."

"Like what?"

"Like every now and then I would blow a little extra wind around Kansas, maybe knocking over a barn or two. Or, I would team up with my Uncle Sun or my cousin Fred Winter, and make everyone crazy with hot and cold air blowing at once. It looked like a storm

69

down on the ground, but believe me, it was just a plain old fit on my part." He laughed again. "Ah, those were the good old days."

"That's way cool," said Junior, flailing his arms in excitement. I wish I could - "

" - Say no more. "I'm going to give you a gift that will help you out in your moments of trouble. Whenever you're in doubt and can't figure things out, repeat these words: Oh Great Wind, I call on you for strength within. I know the importance of family and friends, of respect, and that on me I should depend. I can do anything if I truly believe. If I truly believe."

"That's corny," said Junior, waving his hands in disdain.

The North Wind's voice began to drift away. "Work with me, Junior. If you need me, call me. I'll be there. All you have to do is believe."

"Wait! Don't go yet. Please, I..."

But the North Wind was gone. After standing there for a minute, looking around with uncertainty, Junior laid down and tried to go to sleep.

In the meantime, Rudie was tossing and turning in his bed, dreaming bad dreams. As he did, the Dream Stealers surrounded him, planting confusion and doubt in his heart. They kicked, they punched, they danced, sparring rapidly with his heart. He struggled, trying to fight them off, but then jumped to his feet and still asleep, shouted, "There's no such thing as Santa Claus and Sprinkles! They're just some little kid's dream! They're make believe!"

The Dream Stealers gave each other high-fives and danced away, chanting "We still got it."

When morning finally came, the sun shined brightly through the cave entrance, revealing soft walls filled with colorful drawings of Santa and Christmas Town. There was even a refrigerator in the back of the cave overflowing with home-baked goodies.

As the group was busy rubbing the sleep and the sun out of their eyes, Wiggles jumped up with alarm. "Quick! Search the cave! There's a Dream-Stealer here."

China realized it too as she felt Rudie's dream dying. She flew around him and stared into his eyes. "Fight Rudie! You must fight. Feel what's in your heart. You're the only one who can bring Sprinkles back."

Rudie ignored her, still in a daze from his restless night. But Kisha and Junior were fired up and ready to roll, rousing everyone to go find Sprinkles. Rudie looked at them as if they were from Mars.

"Hey, chill a minute. Did someone put magic dust in your eyes or something?" China was very worried. "Rudie, are you all right?" She searched his face for a clue.

Rudie just shrugged. "Yeah, why? They're the ones who are weird. Look at them. I thought they didn't believe in all this stuff. Did I miss something?"

"I'm afraid something terrible happened to you during the night, Rudie. Do you still believe?" asked China.

Rudie shrugged again. "I guess so."

Hem Wong and China exchanged alarmed glances. They knew they didn't have much time.

Kisha and Junior didn't know what happened. They were too caught up in their excitement and too busy eating the bread they found in the refrigerator. Although it was icicle cold in the refrigerator, as soon as they pulled the bread out it miraculously turned warm and fresh and gooey with melted butter.

"Okay, Rudie Cunningham, you lead. Which way should we go?" Kisha bowed at Rudie.

Junior answered for him, pointing east toward the light. But Rudie insisted they go northwest. Luckily Matt stepped in. "Junior may be right," he said, "That light could be the Ray of Hope."

"Ray of Hope? What's that?" asked Rudie.

Hem Wong explained. "It has been said that the Ray of Hope is created from all the hopes and dreams that exist in the world. It shines bright because the dreams are alive and well. The more people believe and follow their dreams, the brighter the light beams."

"The Dream-Stealers have been trying to put the light out for thousands of years," added Wiggles.

"That's good enough for me!" cried Junior. "To the Ray of Hope and bringing Sprinkles home!"

Everybody gave a shout and followed Junior out of the cave. Everybody except Rudie, that is. He stayed where he was and yelled out, "Hey you guys, think about what you're doing. You're taking directions from Junior. Do you really believe he knows better than me?"

"Well, your way would have taken us back to Christmas Town. With Junior's at least we have a chance," answered Yunnie.

Everyone looked at Rudie. "Are you coming?" asked Junior?"

Rudie was his own self enough to realize he was being selfish and insensitive. "Sure," he said sheepishly, "why not?"

CHAPTER

8

Swallowed Whole

THE GROUP HEADED EAST, through a valley and over hills, until they came to a large black frozen lake. The lake looked mean and impossible to cross.

Rudie smirked. "It looks like a dead end to me, big brother. What do we do now?"

Junior stared across the lake. "Well, um, let me see." Then he made a decision and pointed his fingers straight ahead. "That way."

"Are you nuts?" asked Rudie. "Into the lake? Have you forgotten I can't swim? You better think of a better way."

Junior stood firm, still pointing across the lake. Hem Wong stepped in to help. "It is said that if your heart is pure and without doubt, you may cross the frozen Black Lake safely."

"And if it's not?" asked Kisha.

"Then the ice will open up and swallow you, and you'll drift in limbo forever."

"What's limbo?" asked Kisha.

"It's like being unemployed and not looking for a job, like Uncle Mac," explained Junior.

Junior decided it was time to have a brother-to-brother talk with Rudie, and pulled him off to the side. "What's gotten into you?"

"I don't know," answered Rudie honestly. "Maybe I'm tired or something. We've been looking for Sprinkles for what seems like forever. I don't think we can find her in time for Christmas."

Junior patted his shoulder. "We will, and you'll get that proof you need that all that Christmas stuff is real. You just hang in there."

"Easy for you to say. You don't have Tyrone and all his friends waiting for you when you get back to school." To himself he added, "I'll never be able to show my face in school again—ever!"

So Rudie agreed to cross the lake, and everyone stepped together onto the black ice. Unsure if the lake would really hold them, they took small, light steps on their tiptoes, prepared to run back to the safety of the shore. As they walked, the sky over their heads turned dark, with man-eating clouds falling lower and lower toward the horizon. It got colder too.

"Yo Yunnie, are you sure this lake is frozen solid?" asked Rudie.

"So I've been told," he answered.

"We can't turn back now anyway," said China. "This is the best way, maybe the only way, for us to get to the other side."

Just then they heard a deep, terrifying growl, like a lion caught in a trap. A voice came from within the lake. "Who dares to cross my lake? Go back! This is a big mistake!"

Everyone stopped to listen, frozen on the ice. The voice spoke again. "Leave my lake at once! Go and never return!"

"I hear you loud and clear," said Rudie, speaking down to the ice. "I didn't know this was your lake. You don't have to hit me with a brick twice. I'm out of here!"

But Kisha grabbed his arm before he could run. "Wait!" She looked down at the ice. "Whoever you are, why can't we cross?"

The voice responded after a moment of eerie silence. "Many like you have come before and were lost. Only one pure of heart can make it safely across. Turn back while you still can. Let doubt in your heart keep your feet on dry land."

After pausing for emphasis, the voice repeated, "Now turn back or be lost!"

Everybody stood still except Rudie, who began walking back toward the shore. "Stop right there!" yelled Junior. "We're going to make it across. I know we can do it."

"But you heard the warning," replied Rudie warily, looking back and forth between his family and friends and the safety of the shore.

"I know," said Junior, "but the voice warned about if you have doubt in your heart, and we all believe. Don't we?" he asked. Everyone nodded except Rudie.

"Anyway," continued Junior, "we're already halfway across. If anything was going to happen to us, it would have happened already. Right?"

"I guess," answered Rudie, still unsure.

Junior grabbed his hand and pulled him forward. "So let's get steppin'!" he shouted gleefully.

Rudie pulled his hand free and followed at his own, slower pace. He kept glancing at the ever-shrinking shoreline behind him.

"Rudie, you must pick up the pace," warned Hem Wong.

But suddenly the ice under Rudie's feet began to melt. He looked down in surprise, and yelled up ahead. "Hey, what gives? Guys, the ice is melting."

Everyone quickly looked down but the rest of the ice was solid as steel. They all looked back at Rudie, who was beginning to cry. "You mean to tell me that the ice is only melting under me?"

The reality of Rudie's situation finally got through to the others. Kisha pointed at Rudie's feet and screamed. China flew around and around, too panicked to stay still. "Hurry!" she said, "We must get to the other side before the ice melts or we'll all be lost."

Everyone started running, but with Rudie's very next step the ice opened its gaping black mouth and swallowed him whole. And just as quickly as it opened, the mouth closed and the ice was once again smooth and shiny. There was no trace of Rudie or the spot where he had fallen. He was completely erased from the picture.

As Rudie fell through the icy water of the Black Lake, he could just make out the shadowy figures of Junior and Kisha above the ice. But after a while he couldn't see a thing. He was all alone, tumbling through the stink.

Finally he hit bottom, landing in something gooey and wet. "Ouch!" he yelled, his voice echoing crazily in the vastness. Rudie rubbed his bottom and felt the sticky goo. He sniffed his hands and recoiled in disgust. "Oh man, my best jeans. What is this stuff?"

He looked around, but couldn't see anything.

"Junior? Kisha?" he called hopefully. Nothing. But there was no response from the darkness.

"Okay," he said, trying to reassure himself, "I'm all alone. I can handle that." He snapped his fingers. "It's dark too, real dark." He snapped again. "I've been there too." He nodded his head, agreeing with his own assessment.

"Hey Rudie!" It was Dream-Stealer number 1, but Rudie couldn't see him yet.

"Now I'm hearing strange voices in a dark smelly place. That I don't like." Rudie wrapped his arms around his chest and waited for something.

Something appeared. In the darkness Rudie could make out three figures. "Who's there?" he called out bravely.

"Who's on first?" called back Dream-Stealer number 1.

"I don't care who's where. I just want to know who's here."

"So you want to know who I am?" He laughed. "Well, your wish is your worst nightmare."

The three Dream-Stealers emerged from the darkness and stood in front of Rudie. He stared wide-eyed, recognizing them as his enemies from school.

"Tyrone! Why, you.... You look bad. You know, old and stuff."

Dream-Stealer number 1 laughed again, only it sounded more like a growl. "So when you look at me you see the one you fear most, and you call him Tyrone." He turned to the other two. "I've been called worse."

"You sure have," agreed Dream-Stealer number 2. "Shut up, will you?"

"Sure boss, anything you say."

"Well, I'd sure like to stay and chat, but I've got to find a way out of here," said Rudie.

"Let's take it now, huh boss?" said Dream-Stealer number 3.

"Take what?" asked Rudie, backing up a few steps.

Dream Stealer number 1 did a quick two-step. "It's a little something I've been doing for the last two hundred thousand years or so."

Rudie stared at him as he spoke. His nose began to melt into his face and his lips fell off and his arms got all wiggly. Then all three Dream-Stealers began to change form, and as they did, their evil laughter grew louder and louder.

"I'd like to stay and watch the show, but I see you guys need some time to yourselves," said Rudie. Then he turned and ran blindly away into the darkness.

The Dream-Stealers transformed themselves back into their original goblin-like forms.

"Ahh, that feels much better," said Dream-Stealer number 1, wriggling his short green arms. "All this changing into what people fear most makes me tired."

"And cranky," added Dream-Stealer number 2.

Dream-Stealer number 1 shot him a murderous glare. "It's show time!" he cried.

They began to chase Rudie. Rudie ran fast and had a head start, but was hampered by the sticky stuff on the ground. It was like running on a field of chewed gum. "This could only happen to me," thought Rudie as he ran.

"Go ahead, run," said Dream-Stealer number 1. Turning to the others he added, "I like it best when they fight. Those are the best ones."

"Yeah," agreed Dream-Stealer number 3. "You take his dreams and I'll give him nightmares for the rest of his life."

"No, I got it better," said Dream-Stealer number 2. "Nightmares are nothing. Regret's where it's at. Regret forever."

"Shut up you two and get me that little boy!" shouted Dream-Stealer number 1.

The three Dream-Stealers were closing in on Rudie and he was almost out of steam. But just then, he slipped and fell through a hole in the lake floor. "Again?" he cried as he fell.

But the Dream-Stealers didn't see him and kept on running until they realized he was gone. "Where is he? We lost him," said Dream-Stealer number 2.

"Don't worry," said Dream Stealer number 1 with a smugly evil grin, "As soon as doubt comes back into his heart he'll draw us back to him."

CHAPTER
9

A Voice In Thin Air

RUDY LANDED AT THE BOTTOM of the hole and tumbled onto another puddle of sticky black slime.

"Ouch!" he cried. "Man. I've got to stop falling into this stuff."

He stood up and looked around cautiously, sensing that he wasn't alone. "Who's there?" he ventured quietly.

"Shhh. Over here, quick," came a soft, lilting voice.

"Who's that?" whispered Rudie.

"Keep it down," repeated the voice. "You want them to find you?"

Rudie sensed something moving in the darkness and inched toward the voice.

"How are they going to find me down here?" he asked, then stopped short. "Hey! You could be them..."

"If that's what you want to spend your time thinking, then you just talk a little louder and you'll see what those Dream-Stealers will do to your head."

"My head? What do you mean what they'll do to my head?" He listened closely, but there was no reply.

"Okay, I'm coming," said Rudie, moving again toward the soft voice. He walked right up to it and closed his eyes. Then he held out his hand. "Hi. I'm Rudie Cunningham. Please tell me you don't want anything from my head."

He heard the same softly spoken voice say, "Open your eyes, Rudie." He did. And when he opened his eyes he shouted. "Hey, I know who you are! You're... well...um... you're her, I mean - "

"I'm..."

"You're the littlest reindeer. You're Sprinkles. I'm so glad I found you." Rudie bent over and gave Sprinkles a big hug. "We've been looking for you to bring you home."

Sprinkles just shrugged and turned her back. "So what?" she said like she didn't care. "We've just got to get out of here."

"What's that supposed to mean?" asked Rudie. "We've looked everywhere for you."

"Who's we? I only see you."

"Well, my brother and sister and some friends were helping me look for you. But anyway, I found you. Now we just have to find a way out of here."

Sprinkles' eyes started to fill with tears. "This is limbo," she cried, "there is no way out. And anyway, who said I wanted to go back?"

"You've got to come back," yelled Rudie a bit hysterically. "Christmas won't be the same if you don't."

Sprinkles began to walk away, her shoulders slumped down so that her nose almost touched the floor.

"Wait!" cried Rudie. "Come back here. What do you mean there's no way out and why don't you want to go back? The people of the world need you."

"The people?" Sprinkles snorted disdainfully. "They don't need me. All they care about is themselves and how to spend all the money they make."

"That's why I left Christmas Town," she continued. "All that greed, all that bitterness. I couldn't put up with filling their hearts with the Christmas spirit when they spend the rest of the year playing color wars and damaging the water and the earth. But what really pushed me over the edge was the sight of all those babies dying."

Sprinkles paused for a moment, too teary to continue. When she spoke again, her tears muffled the words. "Those babies, disregarded because their parents didn't care, had no respect for themselves or their unborn children." She shuddered. "So I ran away. But, because I had doubt in my heart, I fell through the Black Lake on my way to the Ray of Hope and ended up in limbo."

Rudie was shocked and scared. "That's bad, Sprinkles," he agreed. "I have to admit, I've never looked at the world like that. But the whole world can't be like that. I can't think of a better place."

Sprinkles looked at him sharply. "Yet here you are. Here we both are. Somehow, we got off track. We didn't listen to what was truly in our hearts. We doubted ourselves, lost sight of our dreams, and then let the Dream-Stealers in to do their dirty work. And now they want to finish the job."

"I knew I shouldn't have crossed that lake," rued Rudie.

"That wasn't your mistake. You gave up hope and so did I. That's why we're both going to be down here in limbo forever, doing nothing but running from the Dream-Stealers now and again."

Rudie covered his ears and then his eyes. He couldn't bear to face the truth. He wished his father was there to tell him what to do. Then he thought about the pictures Santa had shown him of all the sad and hopeless people and he felt a surge of determination. He stood up and looked into Sprinkles' still teary eyes.

"What can we do to change that?" he asked, a new note of confidence in his voice.

"It's not just up to us, Rudie. Everyone on earth has to be more tolerant, treat everyone equally with love and respect. That's what has to happen before anything can change."

Rudie grew impatient. "But what can we do to get out of here now?"

"It's almost impossible," said Sprinkles. "There's only one way. Someone who cares as much as you has to get to the Ray of Hope. And if what's in his or her heart is true, that person can bring us back. But nobody knows we're here."

"Well, somebody knows, but it's my sister and brother," replied Rudie. He felt very glum and hopeless again. He sat down next to Sprinkles and covered his face with his hands.

CHAPTER
10

The Ray of Hope

AS SOON AS RUDIE FELL through the ice, Junior, Kisha and the others started pounding on it desperately, trying to find an opening or any sign of Rudie. Hem Wong finally pulled Junior to his feet. "Junior, he's gone. Come on, there's nothing we can do right now."

"What do you mean nothing?" cried Kisha. "What are we going to do now that both Rudie and Sprinkles are gone?"

"Hold on," said Junior, a new tone of authority in his voice. "Rudie's not lost. He's just not here right now."

The others look puzzled so Junior explained. "Remember what Wong said about not crossing the lake with doubt in your heart? Well, Rudie must have been swallowed up by his doubt."

"I think we should go back for help," said Kisha.

Junior disagreed. "No, that will take too long. We've got to keep going and now look for both of them."

Hem Wong and Wiggles agreed, and then China and the others nodded their agreement as well. So they hurried off the lake as quickly as possible. They came upon the other shore, the one where they had seen the Ray of Hope. Above them, the sky had brightened with rainbow sunshine, boosting their spirits and their hope.

Suddenly, China's light went out and she fell helplessly to the ground. Junior ran over and gently tried to wake her. "China, what's wrong? Wake up."

China stirred softly, able to manage only the barest of whispers. "I'm so weak. I just want to sleep."

"You can't sleep now. We're almost at the Ray of Hope," argued Junior.

"Junior," China tried to explain, "I'm nothing without Sprinkles. I was given life because of her, and if Christmas comes without her, I'll be lost forever."

"Nothing's going to happen to you or to Sprinkles," Junior proclaimed confidently. "I'm sure that Rudie has found Sprinkles by now, and they're both probably out looking for us."

He picked China up gently and put her into his pocket. "You just stay right here," he said softly. "Everything will be okay. You'll see."

Everyone was staring at Junior by now, amazed at his transformation but still doubtful of his words. "What's the problem?" he barked. "I said it will be okay. Now let's go!"

The group trudged forward and soon came upon the Ray of Hope. It was the most beautiful sight they'd ever seen, like a newly sharpened Crayola box of vibrant colors that stretched for miles without end. Junior took China out of his pocket and held her up to the Ray. As she looked, her face reflected the bright colors, and her body slowly came back to life. She felt hopeful again.

"This is certainly a Kodak moment," said Kisha, unable to take her eyes off the Ray of Hope. "Boy, what I wouldn't do to have a picture of this!"

"Wish no more," said Junior. "Today is your lucky day. I just happen to have a camera right here." He reached into his pocket but came up empty. "I know I had it when we went through the closet," he said puzzled.

"Junior, your name should have been H.I.T.H." said Kisha. What does that mean?" asked Wiggles.

"Hole in the head."

Junior ignored Kisha. He remembered the North Wind's invitation and decided it was a good time to test it out. He stepped away from the others and called out to him:

> "Oh Great Wind, I
> call on you for strength
> within. I know the
> importance of family
> and friends, of respect,
> and that on me I should
> depend. I can do
> anything if I truly
> believe. If I truly
> believe."

The North Wind answered immediately; sending swirling gusts down around Junior's head. "Hey, hey Junior, what's up?"

"I thought I had a camera when we started this little outing, but somehow I've misplaced it. Can you give a brother a hand? I mean some help?"

"Is that what you really need?" asked the North Wind with surprise. "A camera? Isn't there something you need that may be a little more important?"

"No, I don't think so," answered Junior. "Just a camera, that's all."

"Okay, a camera you want, then a camera you shall have."

Junior stood with his arms spread out, letting the rays and the wind encircle him. The large, gnarled hands of the North Wind materialized and lifted Junior's hands to his face.

He told Junior, "Just put your finger here like this, point and shoot."

Junior looked doubtful. "Hey, what's this? There's no camera here. What are you trying to do, make me look stupid?"

"There is a camera here," explained the North Wind patiently. The camera is you. Believe what you see and it will be. Just click when you're ready. You'll get real pictures, don't worry."

"How will they develop pictures from a camera they can't see?"

"Relax, Junior. They will. Remember, just believe that it's real and it will be. That's how things work around here. Use your imagination, let yourself go, and you'll feel the power from within. Just believe and everything you want will be."

Junior was so excited with his invisible camera. He ran around everywhere aiming and clicking. "Kisha, look here." Click. "Matt, Yunnie, look at me." Click. "Wiggles, Wong and China, say cheese." Click. "Hey, this is fun. Everybody, hold still."

"Junior Cunningham! Have you blown the last good senses God gave you or did he take them back?" asked Kisha.

"Just hold still. I want one of you by the Ray of Hope."

"It's got to be this place," said Kisha to nobody in particular. "He's losing it; taking pictures with his hands. Man. You see what using your imagination for a full day has done to you?"

"No, Miss Thing, you do anything for a full day -- that's a job. This is fun!"

"Stop all this bickering, you too," admonished Wiggles, "Have you forgotten why we're here?"

"Tomorrow is Christmas," warned China. "I thought that with Rudie we could save Sprinkles in time, but now they're both lost. And my time is - "

" - Wait!" said Wiggles. "What we need is some magic. You know, in all those stories, something magical always happens to save everyone from a tragic end. China, can't you get us out of here?"

"My magic is dying," she replied sadly. "It came from Sprinkles."

"So what do we do now?" asked Hem Wong.

"We've got to keep going. We will find them," said Junior. Then he heard the North Wind whisper to him, "Stand in the rays. It will lead you."

"I think I can do it!" shouted Junior. "I can make everything right. Quick everyone, stand in the rays."

The children and their friends stepped into the Ray of Hope and waited, but nothing happened. They waited more, but still nothing happened.

Everyone was staring at Junior, who was sweating from the bright rays and the stress of being in charge. He finally had to tell them about the North Wind and the help he had promised.

Kisha was skeptical. "Why would he give you this power instead of one of us?" she asked.

"I don't know," admitted Junior. "I guess that's something you'll have to figure out for yourself. But since I was the one who got us here, it makes sense that I'd be the one who could get us out."

"I thought you just fell through the closet," said Hem Wong.

Junior glared at him. "Well, anyway you look at it, I got us to the Ray of Hope."

"Yeah, but Rudie didn't want to cross the Black Lake, and now he's lost too," accused Wiggles.

"I'll admit that everything I've done up to this point hasn't been perfect, but come on, keep working with me. Maybe if we all believe enough that the North Wind can get us back home, then maybe we can get Rudie home too."

"And Sprinkles," added China.

"So all we have to do is believe?" asked Wiggles, who clearly didn't believe.

"Is that what I said?" asked Junior, needing some sort of affirmation from the group.

"That is what I heard," said Hem Wong.

"Then that's it," said Junior, with a big smile now on his face. "All we have to do is believe."

He gathered everyone close to him and asked the North Wind for help once again." Oh Great Wind, I call on you for strength within. I know the importance of family and friends, of respect, and that on me I should depend. I can do anything if I truly believe. If I truly believe."

As Junior spoke, the wind picked up, and great swirls surrounded the group as they huddled together in hope. The Ray of Hope grew brighter. And the colors, blown about by the wind, transformed everything into a circus of vivid hues, which seemed to be alive with movement. Eventually the voice of the North Wind bellowed from the sky.

"Junior, you called?"

"Sorry to bother you, but I need your help again."

"Just tell me and it's yours."

Kisha interrupted with a shout. "Just send me home...now!"

"Ignore her," said Junior, "bad hair day. Anyway, we came here to find Sprinkles, but we didn't, and now my kid brother got swallowed up by the Black Lake so we've lost him too."

"And you'd like to get him back?" asked the North Wind.

"Yeah, we'd like to get him back," yelled Kisha.

"I could send her in his place," offered the North Wind with a sympathetic grin.

"Thanks," said Junior, "but I'd like to keep my family together and get back home." He blinked hard after he spoke, as if his words surprised him.

"Junior, don't forget Sprinkles," reminded China.

"Oh yeah, and could you return Sprinkles to Christmas Town in time for Christmas so she can return the Christmas spirit?" He paused. "I'm not asking too much, am I?"

The North Wind shook his head thoughtfully. "I'll do what I can, but in order to get Rudie and Sprinkles home, they have to want to come home more than anything. It's their hearts, not me, that will do it. But you guys, you're on your way. Just believe."

The sky grew black and then turned bright blue and yellow. The trees shook and the ground cracked as the North Wind rearranged time and space to get the children home. In the midst of all that, the North Wind asked Junior a question.

"Junior, you could have asked to go home a lot sooner. Why didn't you?"

"Cause you gave the power to a kid with no living brain cells," said Kisha.

"Say the word and she stays," offered the North Wind again. He had his own sisters to deal with and was very sympathetic to Junior.

"Nah, I'll take a rain check," said Junior. "I'd just like to get home." He took out his camera and took a few pictures before the whole earth shook and the children disappeared.

CHAPTER
11

A Dead End

MEANWHILE, BACK IN LIMBO, Sprinkles and Rudie weren't having much fun. They felt the earth shaking around them and had to duck when debris from the walls started falling. But when it was all over, they saw a light piercing the darkness in the distance.

"Sprinkles, what's going on?" asked Rudie nervously.

"I don't know. Shhh! I don't think we're alone."

They looked at each other, and at once both jumped up and started running toward the light, thinking they were home-free. Then the Dream-Stealers appeared and began chasing them.

"Why run?" asked Dream-Stealer number 1. "In time I'll get what I want. So let's cut the aerobic training and just give it to me now."

Rudie and Sprinkles ran for their lives. "What do they want from us?" asked Rudie as he ran.

"Your dreams," replied Sprinkles. "Now move!"

As they ran, Sprinkles explained further. "They wear you down, get into your head, and place doubt in your heart. Then they hang around sucking all the life out of you. 'Til you're nothing."

"They'll never get what's in my heart!" declared Rudie.

"Oh, I wish I'd never left Christmas Town," cried Sprinkles. "I want to go home."

"If we can keep ahead of those Dream-Stealers, we'll both get home. I know it!"

They ran even faster, still ducking the falling debris. But the Dream-Stealers stayed close behind.

"What gives with the earth, huh boss?" asked Dream-Stealer number 3 as he ran.

"Feels like the Ray of Hope is doing a number on something," replied Dream-Stealer number 1.

"The last time the earth shook like this, I was just about to steal the dream from a young kid named Michael Jordan. He wanted to be the greatest basketball player ever. And I almost had him, but then the Ray of Hope butted in and I lost him."

"He did become the greatest, didn't he?" offered Dream-Stealer number 2.

"Shut up, will you?" These two will be my all-time prize. I'm going to steal the spirit of Christmas and kill a little boy's dream, both at the same time."

Just as he said that, Rudie and Sprinkles ran into a dead end. They had no choice but to turn and face their enemies.

"Well look what we've got here," said Dream-Stealer number 2, rubbing his hands together in glee.

"Yeah, look what we've got here, Boss," said Dream-Stealer number 3.

"It's the famous Sprinkles, the spirit of Christmas," sneered Dream-Stealer number 1. "And you, home boy," he said, addressing Rudie, "you really thought you could save Christmas?"

His eyes started to glow as he imagined his evil reward.

"You still look a lot like Tyrone," said Rudie.

"Quiet!"

Dream-Stealer number 1 reached for Sprinkles' heart, his head bobbing and his eyes popping, and his skin turning several different shades of purple. But just then, the ground began to shake again and a swirl of wind bursts through the crack of light, encircling Rudie and Sprinkles in a protective shield.

The Dream-Stealers looked at each other in alarm. "Oh no, not again," screamed Dream Stealer number 1, beating number 3 atop his head. "Why does this keep happening to me? Why? They were almost mine!"

"What's going on?" asked Rudie. "I feel all tingly."

"I don't know Rudie, but they don't seem to like it," answered Sprinkles.

The three Dream-Stealers were doing an angry dance, beating their chests and flailing their arms in frustration. Suddenly, the beam of light grabbed Rudie and Sprinkles and they vanished from the spot.

CHAPTER
12

Christmas Morning

AS IF FROM A DREAM, Rudie and Junior awoke in their own beds. Rudie sat up and rubbed his eyes, and Kisha walked in, looking tired and dazed.

"Wow! What happened?" asked Rudie. "I'm in my room now, but I was in... Oh, what am I saying? I'm here in my own bed, everything's the same. It must have been a bad dream." He laid back down. "Yeah, a bad dream."

"Speaking of dreams," said Kisha, "Rudie, I had this dream last night that you wouldn't believe. We were all out looking for Sprinkles and you fell through this

107

Black Lake and were lost forever. All I wanted to do was come home, and then I woke up in my bed. Some bad dream, huh?"

She hugged Rudie, who pulled away. "Hey, what gives?" he said. Not realizing the implication of what Kisha had said.

But then Junior added his own part. "That's strange," he said, "I had almost the same dream, but in mine, I was a hero. After Rudie fell in the lake, I got the North Wind to send us back home. Boy am I thirsty!"

"Him, a hero?" laughed Kisha. "Dream on! That boy just had himself a good old-fashioned nightmare."

"Maybe," said Rudie, looking scared, "but I had almost the same dream."

"Strange, huh?" said Kisha, "all of us having the same dream."

"I'm glad it was just that... a dream," said Junior. "I would have missed the three square meals, free rent, car service, maid and butler service, and the kicker—unlimited free banking. No need to deposit, just pitch a fit now and then, and the vault door swings open." He snapped his fingers. "Just like that!"

He fell back onto his bed, staring up at the ceiling.

But Kisha wanted to talk about the dream. "I wonder if Sprinkles made it home for Christmas."

"I wonder," said Rudie slowly.

"Well, there's only one way to find out," said Junior. "Today's Christmas!"

"The tree!" they all cried in unison and tore out of the bedroom.

When they got downstairs, their parents were waiting for them, sitting amid piles and piles of prettily wrapped gifts. The tree was ablaze with lighted ornaments, red, gold and blue.

Junior and Kisha attacked. Junior put on his new sneakers and Kisha admired herself in her new Santa Claus earrings before Rudie opened even one gift. He just sat down quietly on the ledge under the living room's big picture window and thought about school.

Jeff got up and sat by Rudie. "Hey, what's wrong? It's not like my little man to sit by himself on Christmas day."

"Dad, I'm going to look like a fool when I get back to school."

"Why?"

"Dad, I explained to you what I told Tyrone and the other kids, you know, about Sprinkles."

"Now Rudie..."

"Nobody will believe me now. And I'll have to get a job because the price of mug money goes up as soon as I get back."

"Son, I don't think you should worry about that now. I'm sure everything will be fine. Why don't you just forget about it and enjoy Christmas?"

"But I said I could get proof that Sprinkles was real!"

"Rudie, do you believe she's real?"

"Yeah, but - "

" - So what if a bunch of kids doesn't believe in Sprinkles or Santa Claus? As long as you do, nothing else matters."

"Easy for you to say," said Rudie glumly. "If I show up at school without some kind of proof, those guys will never stop teasing me. It could continue through my formative years. Then what will I have to look forward to? Years of therapy?"

Jeff stifled a smile. "Son, you have nothing to worry about. Every parent tells his or her child some kind of holiday story. Some people believe they're true. Some don't. It doesn't matter. The stories are part of the holiday tradition."

Rudie looked at him through hooded eyes, suddenly having a terrible realization. "So you're saying that you haven't been telling me the truth?"

Jeff realized how serious Rudie was and tried to be honest without causing Rudie to give up his belief. "Well, uh, what I mean is, that we're all Santa's helpers. Your mother and I, like all other parents, work hard to make Christmas nice for our families. Part of that is passing down the stories we heard as children. Most stories have some truth to them, or else they wouldn't survive. So it's up to you to believe it or not. Do you understand?"

"Dad, I know you mean well, but I don't need an explanation. What I really need is a picture of a kid that looks just like me with a small reindeer and an old guy with a white beard that I can put in my backpack and take to school to get Tyrone off my back for a year or two."

Jeff didn't know what else to say, but he hated to see Christmas spoiled for Rudie. "Why don't you try to forget about that just for today, open your presents, and enjoy Christmas? It will be gone before you know it."

Rudie obediently opened up all his presents, but his heart was still heavy.

CHAPTER
13

Junior Takes a Hit

IT WAS TIME to go back to school. With deep sighs and long faces, the three children left their house and began walking. The streets were filled with snow, and they stopped occasionally to throw snowballs at one another.

Just as they approached the schoolyard, Tyrone appeared, flanked by Skippy and Freddy. "Hey, there's our little ornament boy!" sneered Tyrone. "Did Santa and the littlest reindeer show up this year?"

The three of them burst out laughing as Rudie froze in his tracks, looking imploringly at Junior. "Leave him alone, Ty, please," warned Junior.

This made Tyrone laugh even harder. "Ooh! Look what we have here boys and girls. Our littlest friend got himself a genuine hero here. Nice, I like heroes.

Turning to Skippy and Freddy, he asked, "Gentlemen, will you please show these nice people how a tulip looks in the snow?"

"No problem," answered Skippy.

"Yeah, just what he said," agreed Freddy.

"Will you just stop that and do what I said?" yelled Tyrone in exasperation.

Skippy and Freddy charged Junior, knocking him to the ground. Then grabbing him from each side, they shoved him headfirst into a snowbank.

"There now," said Tyrone, "that's beautiful. One down and two to go."

Kisha glared at Tyrone with her best, younger sisters' attitude. "Hold up, home boy! If you think you're going to dump Kisha C. Cunningham headfirst into the snow and ruin my one-of-akind designer outfit, you'd better bring your lunch and a Twinkie 'cause it's going to be a long day!"

Tyrone stared at Kisha in surprise, unsure of how to proceed. Then the school bell rang, and masses of children began walking around them and into the school.

"I guess that means - "

" - Saved by the bell, huh, huh?" said Freddy.

Tyrone threw Freddy a threatening glance then turned to Rudie. "We'll pick this up later, right where we left off."

Rudie and Kisha pulled Junior from the snow and they headed into the school. Junior was embarrassed and angry, and trailed behind his brother and sister. He vowed to get Tyrone for what he'd done.

CHAPTER

14

Do You Believe?

RUDIE'S CLASS WAS FULL, and the teacher Ms. Burzo finally walked in. Without saying a word, she went straight to the blackboard and began writing the day's lesson. Tyrone, Skippy and Freddy sat in the back of the room, making faces at Ms. Burzo and teasing Rudie, who sat right in front of them.

"Just ignore them," advised Pam. "They're so simple."

"Cunningham, I believe you have something you want me to see," whispered Tyrone in a sing-song voice.

Rudie ignored him, so Tyrone raised his voice a bit. "I guess you don't hear so well, Cunningham... Okay, it's time to put up or pay. That's just how it's got to be."

"That's the way it's got to be, right, Ty, huh, huh?" said Freddy.

Tyrone looked like he might slug him, but he just stared him down. "Yeah, Freddy, that's the way."

Rudie turned around. "Shh! I'll show you later," he said, trying to buy time. But Tyrone jumped up and grabbed Rudie by his shirt, lifting him right out of his shoes.

"No way! I want to see what you have and I want it now!"

By now, everyone had turned around and Ms. Burzo raced over to Tyrone. Tyrone was almost as tall as she was and they stood eye to eye for a moment.

"Put him down right now!" she said in her steely teacher voice. "What's wrong with you kids? Back from Christmas break for five minutes and already you're acting like animals. What's going on here?"

Rudie and Tyrone were both silent. Ms. Burzo started yelling. "Why do you kids put each other down and fight all the time?"

She looked around the class. "Somebody tell me something."

Skippy waved his hand in her face. "Ooh, ooh, Ms. Burzo, can I answer that please?"

"Even though I should probably know better, go ahead, tell me what's going on."

Skippy sat up boldly. "As you can see Ms. Burzo, there are three of us who are a tad larger than out fellow classmates, which means that together we become an awesome force. That gives us an edge, or leverage as you may put it, with people like you to ensure that we get a proper education so we can go out and get jobs and stuff and live our lives phat. And maybe if we push these little folks around long enough, we could work our way right up to the White House." Ms. Burzo stared at him with her mouth open and her eyes wide.

"That wasn't too heavy for you, was it, teach? If you'd like, I could break it down."

"No thank you, I've heard all I need. Sit down please."

She pulled Rudie aside and he explained why Tyrone was picking on him. He quickly told her the whole story, aware of Tyrone's eyes boring a hole in his back.

When Rudie was finished, Ms. Burzo asked him gently, "How were you going to prove that?"

"All you adults ask the same question. If I knew the answer, would I be standing here with Tyrone's fingerprints on my collar?"

Ms. Burzo just shook her head. "I'll keep you after school until your brother and sister get here."

"Thanks but no thanks," replied Rudie, looking back at Tyrone. This is my problem and running away won't make it any better. Someday he'll get his. He'll get tired from beating me up and when he's really weak -- POW! - Right in the mouth. Then I'll run like crazy."

Ms. Burzo laughed. "An eye for an eye and a tooth for a tooth isn't always the best way. There's always going to be another Tyrone somewhere."

"Ms. Burzo, for as many times as he's tried to knock my teeth out, I'm looking forward to the day I can have a go at his, no matter how wrong you say that is."

When the school bell finally signaled the end of the day, Rudie gathered his books and walked up to Ms. Burzo's desk. "Thanks for the offer," he said. "I know you were only trying to save my life. I'll wait for my brother and sister outside."

He walked a few steps, then turned back around. "You were kidding about *another like Tyrone* weren't you?"

When Rudie got outside, Pam was waiting for him, along with Junior, and Kisha who were already there. A moment later, so were Tyrone and his goons. The three of them were chanting loudly. "Baby talk, baby talk, you believe in Santa."

"Hey, why don't you pick on someone your own size?" yelled Junior.

"Oh yeah? Like you?" said Tyrone.

"You don't want to get me mad," yelled Junior, praying somebody would come save him.

"You must have a very short memory. How about my buddies here put you back where you started the day, and then nobody has to see you get mad."

"Hey Ty," said Rudie, "it's me you have it in for, so why don't you just leave my family out of it? In fact, why don't you leave us all alone?"

"You want me to leave you alone? Then give me your proof or admit those stories are all made up and you're still a baby."

At this point Kisha realized the dream they all had was real, and she stepped in to defend Rudie. "He did see Santa," said Kisha. "The stories are all true. We were there, all of us."

Freddy turned to Skippy. "Hmm, the whole family's whacked."

"Where's the proof?" repeated Tyrone, getting really angry now.

Rudie looked helplessly at Kisha, who jumped up and smiled. "Junior has it," she said triumphantly.

"I do?" asked Junior.

"You're the one who said you were the hero," said Kisha. "Come on, give the man his proof.

You know, that Ray of Hope stuff."

"What are you talking about?" asked Tyrone, getting puzzled now.

"Yeah?" said Junior, equally puzzled.

Tyrone stepped into Junior's face. "You don't really want to play this game, do you? Give me the proof right now!"

"Go ahead," said Kisha, "give it to him."

"I can't," said Junior. Beads of sweat had freckled his forehead.

"Why not?"

"Cause I don't have the slightest idea of what she's talking about."

"We're dead," said Rudie softly.

"They're dead," said Freddy loudly.

"You said you had a magic camera, remember?"

"But that means the film would be magic too. How will I get it developed?"

Tyrone screamed again. "I've had enough!" You have to the count of ten, and then we're going to take a few magic pictures of our own. One... two...three - "

But while Tyrone was counting, Junior's mind was hard at work. He finally remembered everything and began reciting the chant the North Wind had given him. Suddenly, the sky grew dark and the ground began to shake as the wind got stronger and stronger. Tyrone and his buddies headed for Junior, and he threw his backpack at them to ward off the attack. But before the backpack could hit, all three bullies got blown through the air, landing headfirst in deep snow piles.

Junior heard the North Wind laugh. "Ha, ha! I like that. Man, that felt good."

Junior pointed to the fallen trio. "Hey big guy, did you do that or am I dreaming?"

"I'm as real as they come," answered the North Wind. "But only those who believe can hear me. Why are those boys bothering you?"

"It's my fault," answered Rudie. "I told them I'd get some kind of proof that Sprinkles and Santa and everything else was real." He looked up. "Where are you anyway?"

Tyrone tried to get up, but the North Wind blew another gust at him, and he fell back down, deeper into the snowbank. "Hey, what's the big deal here? Asked Tyrone. "What are you guys doing to us?"
"Yeah," asked Skippy, "what did we do?"

"You have to ask?" said Pam.

"Come on, we were just having a little fun," said Freddy.

Tyrone finally got up, brushing the snow from his body. "I don't know how you did it," he said, "but I'm not impressed. And I don't have time for this mess. Come on guys, let's finish up with the Cunninghams. We've got lunch money to collect."

They headed toward Junior, and once again the North Wind blew them into a snowbank, this time under a huge sign reading "Dead End."

Rudie, Junior, and Kisha laughed and started to walk home. "I guess you guys need a little time alone now, huh?" said Rudie.

"CUNINGHAAAAAAAAMM!" yelled Tyrone.

They continued to walk away and Junior stopped to pick something out of the snow. "Hey sis, you dropped something." He looked at it and his mouth fell open. Kisha looked over his shoulder and turned white.

"Hey, that's me at the Ray of Hope. It wasn't a dream." She looked at the ground. "Hey, there's more."

Suddenly there were pictures everywhere. Three were pictures of Wong, Wiggles, the furballs, and most important, a picture of Rudie with Santa and Sprinkles. As fast as they could collect them, more pictures appeared in the snow.

Rudie took one and shoved it in Tyrone's face. "See, I was telling the truth, but you didn't want to see it 'cause your heart is so twisted and cold. You want to steal other folks' dreams 'cause you have none of your own. I think you really wish you were more like me, but of course you won't admit it and face the pain in your heart. That's why you're destined to go through life backwards."

He tossed the picture to Tyrone. "You can have this. I hope you find yourself before it's too late." Then he turned to Freddy and Skippy. "And you two, get a life!"

"What does he know," blustered Tyrone? "He's just a kid. I'll teach him something as soon as I get out of here."

Skippy reached for a picture in the snow. It showed him and Tyrone sitting under the "Dead End" sign. "Just you and me, Ty."

"Where am I?" asked Freddy.

"Don't know," answered Tyrone. "Hmm, it's not a bad shot." He turned to Skippy. "Do you think they got my good side?"

"Hey," said Freddy, "let me see that. I got to be somewhere in there. We're always together."

Tyrone and Skippy ignored him, still staring at the picture. "Yo, Ty man," said Skippy weakly, "I don't think you have a good side here. Look. We both look bad, kind of homely." He looked closer. "We look homeless!"

Tyrone laughed. "Man, look at us. That's bad, ain't it."

Neither Skippy nor Freddy saw the humor, but Freddy laughed because Tyrone did. He asked again, "How come I'm not in the picture?"

"Gee Freddy. I don't know. Maybe you're dead or something," said Tyrone.

"Or maybe your mama got her wish and you got sent away," said Skippy.

Freddy picked himself up and walked away, then turned back. "Yeah, well maybe I'm in school trying to make something out of my life."

"Yo homes, where you going?" called Skippy.

"To find some of those people I've hurt since I've been hanging out with you two losers.

Maybe they'll forgive me and give me a second chance."

Skippy jumped up and ran after him. "Yo, homey, wait up. Me too."

"Hey you two, get back here," yelled Tyrone. He tried to get up but kept falling back down. "Hey, come here and help me. Where are you going?"

"I don't know, dude," answered Skippy, "but I don't like the way I looked in that picture, so wherever I go, it's got to be better than where you're headed."

Freddy said to him, "Yo Ty?"

"What?"

"Don't ever tell me to shut up again?" Then he ran to catch up with Rudie.

As Skippy and Freddy ran away, Tyrone kept trying to get up, but with no luck. He kept falling back to the ground. All around him were pictures of Rudie, Sprinkles, Santa, and happy people all over the world celebrating Christmas.

"What do they know?" fumed Tyrone, still trying to claw his way out of the snow. "You don't get second chances. It doesn't work that way. People like me RULE! Maybe next year I'll be taking their lunch money."

Tyrone was left alone, sitting helplessly in the snowbank. Freddy and Skippy were walking with Rudie, laughing like old friends. The air was calm, the sky was blue, and the world looked very pretty. A single picture blew through the air, settling on a soft patch of ground at the bottom of a slide in the playground. It showed

Rudie with Santa, Sprinkles, China, Wong, Wiggles, Matt, Yunnie and the furballs. Across the bottom was written, "DO YOU BELIEVE?"

THE END

About the Author

Author, Lifestyle Coach, and Professional Trainer, P. Kevin McLemore is constantly challenging himself to be his best version possible. A family man first, much of McLemore's success in his personal and professional life is owed to the motivation gleaned from fatherhood as well as beautiful moments shared with his supportive wife, Monika. A masterful and prolific writer, McLemore is looking forward to the 2019 release of his non-fiction book, **Dating With a Full Deck**.

Keep in touch with
P.Kevin McLemore
pkmclemore@aol.com